PENGUIN WORKSHOP
An imprint of Penguin Random House LLC
1745 Broadway, New York, New York 10019

First published in the United States of America by Penguin Workshop,
an imprint of Penguin Random House LLC, 2025

Copyright © 2025 by Tara J. Hannon

Penguin supports copyright. Copyright fuels creativity, encourages diverse voices, promotes free speech, and creates a vibrant culture. Thank you for buying an authorized edition of this book and for complying with copyright laws by not reproducing, scanning, or distributing any part of it in any form without permission. You are supporting writers and allowing Penguin to continue to publish books for every reader.

PENGUIN is a registered trademark and PENGUIN WORKSHOP
is a trademark of Penguin Books Ltd, and the W colophon is a
registered trademark of Penguin Random House LLC.

Visit us online at penguinrandomhouse.com.

Library of Congress Cataloging-in-Publication Data is available.

Manufactured in China

ISBN 9780593753149 (pbk)   10 9 8 7 6 5 4 3 2 1 HH
ISBN 9780593753156 (hc)   10 9 8 7 6 5 4 3 2 1 HH

Design by Aya Ghanameh

This book is a work of fiction. Any references to historical events, real people, or real places are used fictitiously. Other names, characters, places, and events are products of the author's imagination, and any resemblance to actual events or places or persons, living or dead, is entirely coincidental.

The publisher does not have any control over and does not assume any responsibility for author or third-party websites or their content.

To my sisters, Paige and Kelsey, my two favorite weirdos. You are where I belong. I love you so much.

Table of Contents

CHAPTER 1:
Horrifying News . . . . page 1

CHAPTER 2:
The Reasons . . . . page 8

CHAPTER 3:
RIP Fun . . . . page 13

CHAPTER 4:
Ghoul at School! . . . . page 18

CHAPTER 5:
Accidental Haunting . . . . page 23

CHAPTER 6:
BOO! . . . . page 31

CHAPTER 7:
The Answer to My Nightmares . . . . . . page 37

CHAPTER 8:
Still Grossie Ghostie . . . . page 43

CHAPTER 9:
Just Like a Human . . . . page 48

CHAPTER 10:
Show-and-Yell . . . . page 53

CHAPTER 11:
Eye Scream . . . . page 64

CHAPTER 12:
Weirdos . . . . page 71

CHAPTER 13:
Gold Star Ghostie . . . . page 79

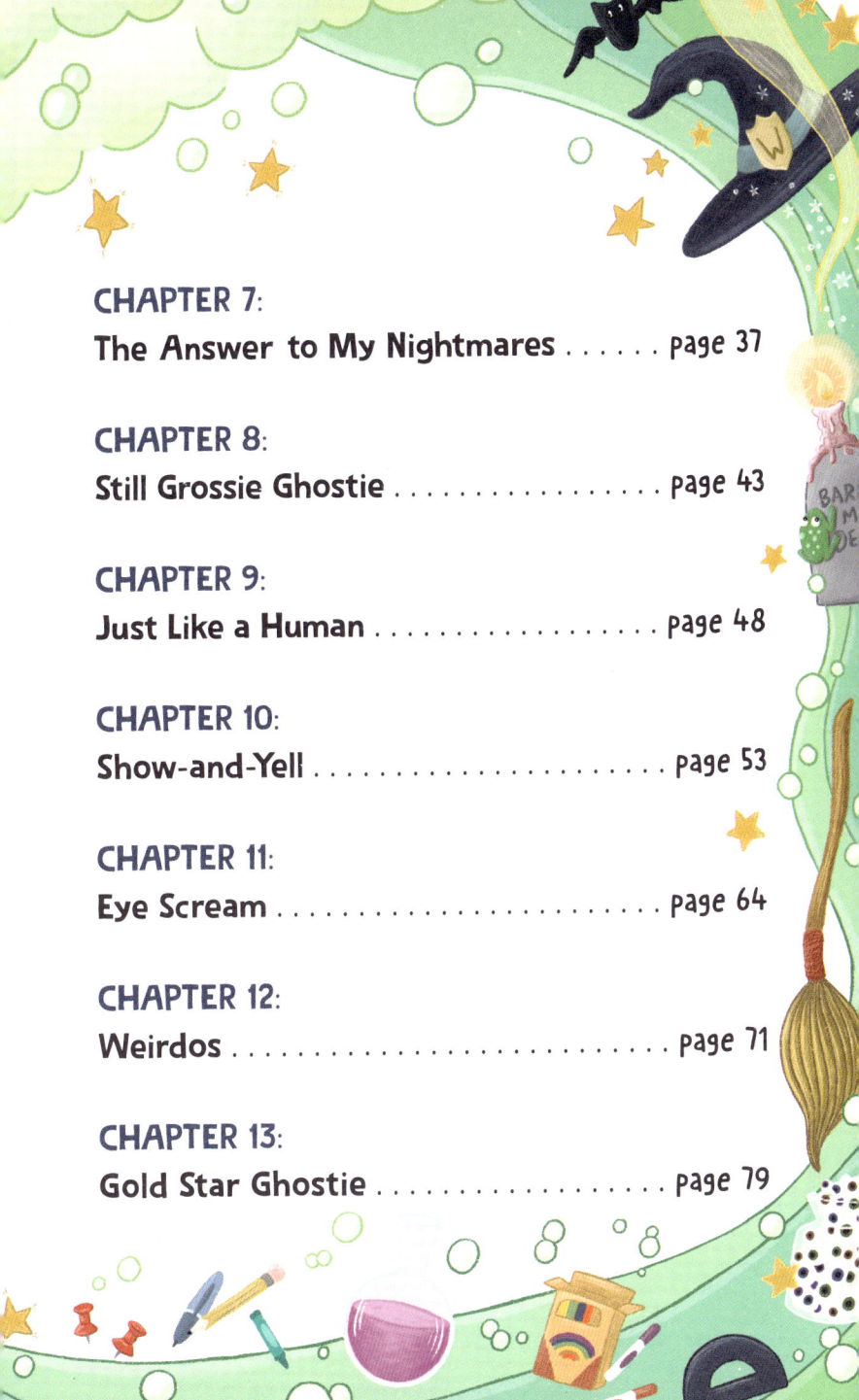

CHAPTER 1

Horrifying News

In Scareville, life was perfectly normal. My friends were witches and werewolves, my house was haunted, and we celebrated birthdays in the best way possible, with scare parties. Until one eerie Tuesday, Mom and Dad ruined everything.

"We're moving to Smithville," they announced at dinner.

"A human town?! But **WHY**?" I moaned.

"I got my dream job as a haunted relations ghoul, or as they say in Smithville, a human relations agent!" Mom said proudly.

"Can you believe it?" Dad shrieked. "We are going to be floating among humans! It's a dream come true!"

My parents are obsessed with humans; they read their books,

follow their news,

and binge-watch their TV shows, but I never thought they would take it *this* far. A ghost family living among **HUMANS**? It's unheard of!

Scareville is a very diverse town filled with ghosts, witches, vampires, skeletons, mummies, monsters, and werewolves... but *never* humans.

"Aren't humans scared of ghosts?" I asked, hoping it would bring my parents back to their senses.

"That's why my job is so important," Mom said. "We have to bridge the gap between the made-up ghost stories and the real ones."

"Will I have to switch schools?" I asked.

"Yes, honey boo," Mom said. "You're already signed up to attend Smithville Elementary. Your teacher is very excited to have you in his class."

"Booooo," I cried.

"Cheer up, kid," Dad said while he rubbed noogies on my head like the human dads do on TV. "Scareville will always be just a haunt away."

"And you're going to love Smithville," Mom said. "I just know it!"

I hoped my mom was right.

CHAPTER 2
The Reasons

She was wrong. Very, very wrong.
I do *not* love Smithville for so many reasons.
Let me count the ways.

REASON NUMBER ONE

Our new house isn't haunted. It is just a normal house with blue shutters that don't rattle and wooden floorboards that don't creak. It's so quiet here! I haven't had a good night's sleep since we moved in a week ago.

REASON NUMBER TWO

On our first night here, I threw Mom a very supportive congratulations-on-your-new-job scare party and she totally freaked out. She vacuumed up all my spider confetti and shrieked, "We can't throw scare parties here! We will scare the neighbors!" Which makes no sense because the whole point of scare parties *is* to scare the neighbors! **RIP** fun.

REASON NUMBER THREE

I can't let Cookie out to catch her dinner at night because there's a leash law here. I don't know what a leash law is, but Dad says it means Cookie has to stay inside unless she's on a leash. She hates that. So do I.

CHAPTER 3

RIP Fun

On the morning of my first day of school, Mom and Dad floated me to the bus stop. Luckily there were no other kids there, because Dad was totally geeking out.

"Do you think the bus will be yellow!?" he asked. "Can I float onto it with you to have a peek or a sniff . . . ? I heard they smell like crayons and old ketchup! Eeeeee! School buses are so . . . human!"

"Daaaaaaad," I groaned. "Please don't embarrass me." I had

never been on a school bus before. In Scareville, everyone used school hearses, broomsticks, or wings if they had them, so I was a little (okay, a lot) nervous to ride the bus. And Dad was making it so much worse.

"Come on, it will only be for a second, you'll barely notice me," he nudged.

I rolled my eyes. "I think I'm gonna puke."

"Bats in your belly, honey?" Mom asked. "No need to be nervous, my little ghoul. The humans are going to love you."

"Humans are scared of ghosts, Mom," I said without hiding my frustration. I hate that I have to keep reminding her of this. "And they won't like being afraid of their classmate."

Mom jiggled my cheeks in her hands

like she did when I was a baby ghost and said, "I know, honey boo, but how could anyone not like being scared by this sweet little face?" Then she added, "You're going to have a great first day!"

I wanted to believe her. But how did *she* know? She had never started at a new school in the middle of the year, with a class full of kids who believed in scary ghost stories. When the bus came, I boarded it without issues and without Dad. Thank goodness.

The bus ride was quiet. Really quiet.

When we finally arrived at school, the human kids ran down the bus steps and in through the giant doors of the school without a single care. I, however, had *a lot* of cares.

The bus driver looked at me in the rearview mirror. "Don't forget to breathe, kid," he said, then added, "You do breathe, don't you?"

I nodded and took a deep breath. Then I slowly floated down the bus stairs and let the giant double doors of Smithville Elementary swallow me up.

CHAPTER 4

Ghoul at School

Inside, I imagined the halls would be filled with kids high-fiving and running to class, but to my surprise, they were empty. I was alone, and apparently, running late. I took another deep breath.

There were four hallways to choose from and I chose the wrong one, twice. I panicked and did what I would have done at Scareville Elementary.

I took a shortcut.

Note to self, learn the school layout before taking shortcuts. Ending up in a toilet within the first five minutes of my first day of school was really bad. Having someone witness it ... was much, *much* worse.

Luckily, the bell rang and the kid ran off before we were forced to make conversation. Unluckily, when I finally floated into my class, he was there telling my teacher everything.

"And then he popped out of the toilet!" he said, loudly enough for everyone to hear.

My teacher patted him on the back. "I'm sorry, that must have been scary for you, Kevin."

Kevin wiped his tears. "I wasn't scared! It was gross—that's why I'm telling you.

He is a gross ghost!" Then he pointed a grubby finger at me and yelled, "He's a Grossie Ghostie!"

"Kevin," my teacher said sternly, "that is not how we treat our classmates!" Then my teacher turned to me. He looked nervous but he did his best to make me feel welcome. He reached out his hand and with a shaking voice said, "Ghostie! It's so nice to meet you. I'm your teacher, Mr. Jones."

"Hi" was all I said, because my voice was shaking, too.

Mr. Jones led me to the front of the class while everyone stared. He stood beside me and introduced me like I was a normal kid even though we all knew I wasn't. "Good morning, everyone," he said. "Today we have a new friend joining our class. Say hello to Ghostie."

I waved as I hovered awkwardly in front of my new human classmates. Only one kid waved back. Ugh. It was a total nightmare and not the good kind.

CHAPTER 5

Accidental Haunting

The rest of my day wasn't any better. In gym class, Ms. Reedy rolled out a bin of rubber balls and shouted, "Two-minute warm-up!" Before I could ask what a warm-up was, a kid threw a ball at me from across the gym.

"Catch!" she yelled.

As the ball came flying in my direction, all I could think was, *Ghosts can't catch!* But it was too late—the ball was already halfway to me. So I did what the other kids were doing and put out my hands. That was pointless. The ball went right through me and bonked a boy named Tate on the head!

"I'm so sorry!" I yelped. But I'm not sure he heard me. He spent the rest of gym in the nurse's office and I spent it on the sidelines.

Lunch was even worse. Becky fainted when she saw me eat my french flies. I felt terrible about it. But I can't help that I am see-through. On the plus side, I got the chance to apologize to Tate.

"I'm sorry my ball hit you in gym class," I said. "I should have warned you. Things go right through me when they are moving fast."

"It's okay," Tate said with a shrug. "I don't really like gym, anyway."

"I thought all humans liked gym," I said.

"Meh." Tate shrugged again. "I'd rather read."

"Oh," I said, a little surprised, and wondered if he had ever read the Ivy and Scream series.

Then the bell rang for recess. My chat with Tate gave me the boost of confidence I needed to introduce myself to some other kids.

Outside, a bunch of kids were playing hide-and-seek, which is one of my favorite games.

So I joined them.

I was doing great!

But after a while, I couldn't find anyone, anywhere …

When I finally found them they looked *really* surprised to see me.

"Wow, you guys are **REALLY** good at hiding!" I said. "It took me forever to find you."

They all screamed, **"RUUNNN!"**

I thought we were still playing so I chased after them.

"I'm gonna get you!" I booed.

But Mr. Jones stopped me. "I'm sorry, Ghostie, you just can't haunt your classmates," he said. "I have to send you to the principal's office."

Principal Williams gave me a sorry smile and sent me home early because haunting classmates is against school rules. I guess I should have been upset because I wasn't really *trying* to haunt anyone, but I was thrilled.

Mom was *not* thrilled. She talked the whole way home about how I can't haunt my friends and how I have to respect human rules and blah blah blah. Luckily, there was still a wad of toilet paper in my ear from this morning, so I jammed it in a little farther until we got home.

CHAPTER 6
BOO!

The next morning, I faked the flu. Humans hate the flu. And Mom says we have to respect human rules, so she would never make me go to school if I was sick with the flu!

"I don't feel so good," I said in my sickliest voice. I coughed and wheezed and burped and sneezed. I even turned a little bit green.

But Mom saw right through me. She said, "Nice try, but ghosts don't get the flu." And made me go to school anyway.

I was totally bummed until I got to school and found out it was Tate's birthday.

"We are going to throw Tate a surprise party," Mr. Jones whispered to the class while Tate was in the bathroom. I watched excitedly while Becky rushed to set out trays of tiny little cakes called cupcakes, Kevin and Neil hung streamers haphazardly around the window, and Mr. Jones blew up a giant balloon that looked just like my second cousin, Gilda. Surprise parties looked like fun!

In Scareville, we celebrated birthdays with scare parties. At my last scare party, I won musical scares three times, and my friend, Skelly, pinned her eyeball on Dad, twice, during pin your eyeball on the zombie.

For the first time in a long time, I was feeling excited. So excited that I *almost* forgot I hated school. I gathered up a little scare party surprise for Tate. Luckily, Mom packed some eyeballs in my lunch and the cabinet under the sink was loaded with spiders. I was ready to party!

I thought surprise parties would be just like scare parties!

I WAS WRONG. VERY WRONG.

Because of me, our classroom was covered in cupcakes and crawling with spiders. Becky fainted, **AGAIN**. And Mr. Jones was unable to teach for the rest of the afternoon. It turns out there is one thing humans hate more than the flu— it's spiders.

I really should have stayed home.

CHAPTER 7

The Answer to My Nightmares

That night, Mom cooked my favorite dinner, frog nuggets and stench fries. But even my favorite nuggets couldn't pull me out of my franken-funk.

"How was your day, honey?" Mom asked.

"I don't want to talk about it," I said.

"Okay," she said softly, then turned to my dad. "How was your day, dear?"

"Fantastic!" my dad responded. "Burt invited me to watch football with him next week, so I got this cool foam finger to bring along!"

"A giant finger?! How delightful!" my mom gushed.

Watching my mom and dad smile at each other made me even grumpier. I hated how happy they were. And I hated how easy it was for them to be ghosts in a human town.

When Dad reached for more nuggets, I watched his tie drag across the ketchup. It looked just like blood! I waited for him to make a funny vampire joke, like "What's a vampire's favorite kind of tie? **TIE DIE**!" His vampire jokes are the best. But all he said was, "A food stain on my tie? Boo-ya! This is such a human problem to have!" Mom and Dad giggled proudly together. It was so gross.

Then it hit me like a cauldron of bricks. Even my *parents* liked humans better than ghosts. The answer to all my problems was suddenly clear. I needed to be more like a human.

After dinner, I asked Mom if she would take me shopping. She loves human stores so she said, "Abso-**BOO**-tely!" We went to a place called the thrift store. It was filled with all kinds of human treasures: shoes, clothes, books, hats, toys, and even fake hairdos! Mom said I could get whatever I wanted. So I got everything!

When we got home, Dad and I learned how to play catch with my new glove and I tried on all my new things! I felt good in my new human outfit! But I knew if I wanted to make friends in Smithville, I needed to change more than just my look.

So I changed...

...my name.

...my lunch.

...and my attitude.

Watch out, Smithville Elementary, there's a new human in town!

CHAPTER 8
Still Grossie Ghostie

When I got to school, I knew I had nailed my new look when I saw that I was wearing the **SAME** shirt as Kevin, who is the *coolest* kid at Smithville Elementary. Everyone noticed! It was awesome.

Mr. Jones remembered to call me Gerald and the rest of the kids... well, they didn't really call me anything at all, which I guess is better than Grossie Ghostie.

Everything was going great until science. It was lab day. Mr. Jones put three paper clips and three magnets on our desks. Then he announced in a spooky voice, "Today we will defy gravity." A chill of shame ran through my body because he made it sound like defying gravity was something *weird*, even though I defied gravity every day by floating.

I closed my eyes and focused on sinking as far down onto my stool as I could. When I opened them, Tate was sitting across from me.

"Boo!" he said, handing me a pair of goggles. "Mr. Jones said we were lab partners."

"Oh. Cool," I said, jamming the goggles onto my head a little too quickly. When they shot across the room, I thought I would die of embarrassment.

But somehow, only Tate saw.

And he laughed. Thank ghoulness.

"Nice shot," he said.

I didn't have the heart to tell him it was an accident, so I just said, "Thanks."

Tate was a good lab partner. We used our magnets to make paper clips float in midair! It was really cool. Until Kevin covered one of his paper clips up with a used tissue and yelled, "Look, Grossie Ghostie can dance!"

Mr. Jones told Kevin to knock it off, but it didn't matter.

Nothing anyone did mattered. I was always going to be Grossie Ghostie.

CHAPTER 9

Just Like a Human

The next morning, I felt lost in a fog. Part of me wanted to stay hidden forever, but then I remembered it was show-and-tell day at school and I had prepared the most perfect, most human-y

show-and-tell item ever—a baseball glove. Dad and I had been practicing and I was getting quite good. There was no way I was going to miss the chance to prove to everyone that I could catch a ball now, just like a human.

It was hard for me to be patient while everyone presented. I fiddled with my carpet square while Becky talked in horrifying detail about her favorite stuffed otter.

I practiced taking deep breaths while Neil talked for twelve whole minutes about his vintage marble set. The deep breaths stopped working about nine minutes into Neil's presentation, so I held my breath instead. (Luckily, ghosts can hold their breath a lot longer than humans.) I was about to lose my marbles on Neil when he finally finished talking and I exhaled. Phew!

Tate was next and then it would be my turn. Tate sat down in the sharing chair carefully holding his show-and-tell item.

No one was ready for what he had in his hands.

No one except me.

CHAPTER 10

Show-and-Yell

When Tate sat the little travel cage on his lap, the whole class scooted away from him, but Tate didn't notice. He reached his hand inside the cage and proudly pulled out a giant, brown, hairy, eight-legged tarantula! It was bigger than his hand!

The whole class gasped.

Becky screamed.

"This is my pet spider, Harry," Tate said.

I had never seen a more beautiful spider in my entire life.

"He is a Colombian giant taran—" Tate tried to continue, but before he could finish, Becky fainted. Which wouldn't have been a problem if she hadn't landed

on Neil, who then spilled his marbles—everywhere!

Mr. Jones ran to help Becky, but he slipped on Neil's marbles and rolled right into Tate. When Tate and Mr. Jones collided, Tate's hands flew into the air and so did Harry.

The giant spider soared over Becky, past Neil, and ...

...landed directly on Kevin's head!

I have never heard a human scream so loud.

Kevin shook his head wildly and flung Harry to the ground. Harry ran to safety under Mr. Jones's desk, and all the kids, including Becky, who was standing upright again, ran out of the classroom.

"Sorry, Ghostie—er, Gerald," Mr. Jones said with a pale face, "but we will have to postpone your show-and-tell presentation to tomorrow." Then with wobbly knees, he bent over and peered under his desk. He swallowed loudly and said to Tate, "I'll need to take Becky to the nurse's office. Can you take care of *that*?" He pointed to Harry.

Tate looked a little wobbly in the knees as well. "Yes, I'm so sorry," he muttered. But Mr. Jones was already halfway to the nurse's office.

I don't think Tate knew I was still in the classroom when he started to cry, so I stayed quiet.

I didn't want to scare him. He kicked the trash can over, then took a deep breath and picked it back up again. That's when I hovered beside him to let him know I was there.

"Well, *that* escalated quickly," I said.

He looked at me and wiped his eyes. "I ruin everything," he said, then sniffled.

"I know exactly how you feel," I said and handed him a tissue. "If it makes you feel *any* better, your presentation was the most exciting show-and-tell I have *ever seen*."

I didn't mean for what I said to be funny, but Tate laughed. Which made me laugh. So we laughed together.

I helped him get Harry out from under Mr. Jones's desk.

Then I let Harry crawl around in my hands. "Harry is really cool!" I said.

"Thanks, I think so, too," Tate said. "Everyone else thinks he's weird."

I just shrugged because I didn't know what to say to that.

No one came back to the classroom for a bit, so Tate and I talked while we waited. He asked me about Scareville and told me that he looked like a werewolf when he was a baby. I told him to prove it, so he promised he would bring in a baby picture of himself.

I was feeling really good after hanging out with Tate. But Kevin ruined it all on the bus ride home when he got everyone to sing thirteen rounds of "The ghost in the toilet goes *swish*, *swish*, *flush*!" at the top of their lungs.

I was mortified.

I wanted to vanish, vanish, vanish.

CHAPTER 11

Eye Scream

When I got home, I launched myself through the front door and cried, "Being a ghost is the worst!" I threw my backpack across the room just as Dad walked in. It went right through him. Oops.

He ignored my airborne backpack, then said in an annoyingly cheery voice, "Well, I think being a ghost is the best."

I slumped onto the couch and blurted, "I'd rather be a booger."

Dad hovered his hand over my shoulder and said, "Being a ghost is a very special thing, son."

"You're a liar," I said. "I know you and Mom wish we were human."

My dad winced. "Wait? You think we want to *be* humans?!" he asked. "Ghostie, we love being ghosts!"

"But you think humans are **SO** amazing." I sniffled.

"Well, I can't pretend that's not true," Dad said. "They really *are* amazing. Today I learned that they have five toes on *each* foot, with little toenails that they trim with tiny clippers. You can't make that stuff up!"

"Ugh! This is exactly what I'm talking about!" I groaned.

"Okay. I see what you are saying," Dad said. "But, Ghostie, I am proud of being a ghost and you should be, too."

My mom appeared through the dining room wall and patted me softly on the hand. "What your dad is *trying* to say is, you're perfect just the way you are."

"Yeah." My dad nodded. "That's exactly what I was saying."

"Thanks, I guess," I grumbled.

"Now, who wants eye-scream sundaes?" Mom asked. Dad and I both raised our hands. While Mom covered our big globby scoops of eye scream with chocolate sauce, Dad pulled some old family albums out from under the couch.

"You come from a long line of very cool ghosts," he said.

"Like who?" I asked.

Dad patted the couch next to him and cracked open a dusty album filled with old photos. "Cozy on up here, little spirit."

I spent the rest of the night eating eye scream and listening to Mom and Dad tell ghost stories about our family. Dad puffed up proudly when we got to a photo of Uncle Ted. "Did you know he spent two terms in the White House as the resident ghost?"

"Uncle Ted haunted the White House?" I asked. "I had no idea."

"Oh yes, he was quite a jokester, too," Dad said. "One Thanksgiving he made it look like the turkey was dancing on the table! Can you imagine seeing Uncle Ted dancing with a giant roasted turkey on the president's fancy dishes?" Dad snorted. "The human news was buzzing with rumors for weeks that the White House was haunted!"

My dad laughed so hard telling this story, he had to pass the album to my mom.

She told me about my great-aunt Betty, who was the first ghost on the moon! "Your great-aunt Betty taught Neil Armstrong how to float without gravity!" she said. "Her role with NASA did wonders for human-ghost relations, unlike the antics of Uncle Ted," she said, rolling her eyes playfully at Dad.

"That is really cool!" I said.

I learned so many other cool ghost stories about my family, but the coolest one was that my second cousin, Gilda, is a ghostwriter for the Pirates of the Scareibbean books. I *love* those books!

Later that night when Mom tucked me into bed, I confessed, "I miss Scareville."

She kissed me on my forehead and said, "I miss Scareville, too, honey boo." And somehow, that made me feel a lot better. "We'll visit soon," she promised.

Before she turned off the light, she loosened one of my floorboards.

It creaked all night long.

I slept great.

CHAPTER 12

Weirdos

The next day, I felt more like myself and I was ready to try again. I was almost out the door when I remembered that I still had to give my show-and-tell presentation. I hovered over the coffin table, staring down at our old family photos, and a rush of excitement crept over me. I yanked the baseball glove out of my backpack and replaced it with my family photo album. I took a deep breath and rushed out the door before I could change my mind.

I was floating into school a few inches higher than usual, humming the tune to "Monster Mash" when I heard Tate's voice yell, "Cut it out, Kevin!"

I rushed toward him and found that Kevin was throwing all of Tate's books and papers into the air. "You threw that spider at me on purpose!" Kevin yelled.

"It was an accident!" Tate yelled back.

I don't know what I was thinking when I floated in between them and yelled, "Stop it!" But I used my spookiest voice and it worked. Kevin froze . . . for a minute. Then he just started laughing. Humans really do laugh at the strangest times.

While Kevin laughed, I searched the ground for reinforcements and found just what I was hoping for. I shot Tate a knowing glance and plucked a big, beautiful daddy longlegs from the rock beside me. It made itself comfortable in my hand as I moved closer to Kevin. "Have you met my friend, Mr. Longlegs?" I asked.

Kevin stopped laughing. His eyeballs looked like they were going to pop out of his head as I leaned the creature even closer. Behind me, Tate lifted a centipede from his muddy math book and smiled.

"Have you ever noticed that the more legs an insect has, the more it tickles on your skin?" Tate asked.

"I wouldn't know," I said. "My ghostly skin can't feel its tiny legs."

Tate laughed.

I laughed.

This time, Kevin did not laugh. "You guys are so weird!" he said.

"You think *one* spider is weird," I said. "You should see my whole collection!"

And without missing a beat, Tate said, "Oh! A spider collection would make a **GREAT** show-and-tell presentation!"

"How many spiders are in your collection?" Kevin asked nervously.

"Three hundred eighty-seven as of yesterday," I said. "But there are a few egg sacs close to hatching, so that could change *very* quickly."

Kevin looked spooked. He turned to Tate and sputtered, "I'm sorry I threw your things." Then he ran as fast as he could away from us.

When I helped Tate collect his muddy books and papers, he smiled at me and said, "Thanks for your help, weirdo."

I smiled back and said, "Anytime, weirdo." Then we both collapsed to the ground laughing. Maybe being weird isn't all that bad.

CHAPTER 13

Gold Star Ghostie

At lunch, Tate showed me his baby picture. "Oh. My. Ghost! You **DID** look like a werewolf as a baby!" I said.

"I told you!" Tate laughed. "My nickname was Little Wolf!"

"I have never seen a baby with that much hair!" I said. "And I've seen *actual* werewolf babies!"

Tate laughed, then howled like a wolf in the middle of the cafeteria!

Everyone stared at us, but we didn't care, because we were laughing so hard. Tate even laughed so hard, milk came out of his nose. I didn't know humans could do that! It was awesome.

I didn't wear my shirt to school today but it didn't really matter because I wasn't nervous to eat in front of Tate. In fact, I showed him a trick, and he loved it!

After lunch, Mr. Jones gave me a chance to do my show-and-tell presentation since I wasn't able to yesterday. I was a little nervous to present. But then I remembered that my stories were *really* cool!

So I told my classmates the ghost stories that I was proud of. I showed them pictures of my family and I even told them about Skelly pinning her eyeball on Dad at my last scare party. Then I made some friendly ghost noises, and Tate howled softly with me from the carpet. Some kids looked a little nervous, others listened excitedly.

And everyone had questions when I was done.

Do ghosts poop?

Can you get sunburned?

Why don't you wear any pants?

Do ghosts eat people?

Do you like rock and roll?

Afterward, Mr. Jones gave me a gold star. He thanked me for sharing my stories and said he learned a lot of new things about ghosts.

Since then, Becky has stopped fainting around me and no one has called me Grossie Ghostie, not even Kevin!

I'm still getting used to being the only ghost in a human school.

But I have found one thing that I really like about Smithville, so I'll be sticking around for a while.